Goodbye Summer!

Kaela Barnett Lewis

This is a work of fiction. All of the characters, names, incidents, organizations, and dialogue in this novel are either the products of the author's imagination or are used fictitiously.

AuthorHouse™
1663 Liberty Drive
Bloomington, IN 47403
www.authorhouse.com
Phone: 1 (800) 839-8640

Because of the dynamic nature of the Internet, any web addresses or links contained in this book may have changed since publication and may no longer be valid. The views expressed in this work are solely those of the author and do not necessarily reflect the views of the publisher, and the publisher hereby disclaims any responsibility for them.

Any people depicted in stock imagery provided by Getty Images are models, and such images are being used for illustrative purposes only. Certain stock imagery © Getty Images.

This book is printed on acid-free paper.

ISBN: 978-1-7283-4883-4 (sc)
ISBN: 978-1-7283-4882-7 (e)

Library of Congress Control Number: 2020907842

Print information available on the last page.

Published by AuthorHouse 05/20/2020

authorHOUSE

Goodbye Summer!

Kaela Barnett Lewis

Londyn and Maxson may the little things
bring inspiration to your lives.

Darius, thank you for dreaming with me.

Larry, Rosiland and Kimberly for
supporting everything, always.

As our summer vacation comes to a close

We're sitting on the beach with the sand between our toes

"Time flies when you're having fun"

This is especially true in the summer sun.

I'm going to miss the long days spent at the park

And miss gazing at the stars in the pitch black dark

I'm going to miss splashing for hours in the big wet pool

Just to beat the heat while my friends and I try to stay cool

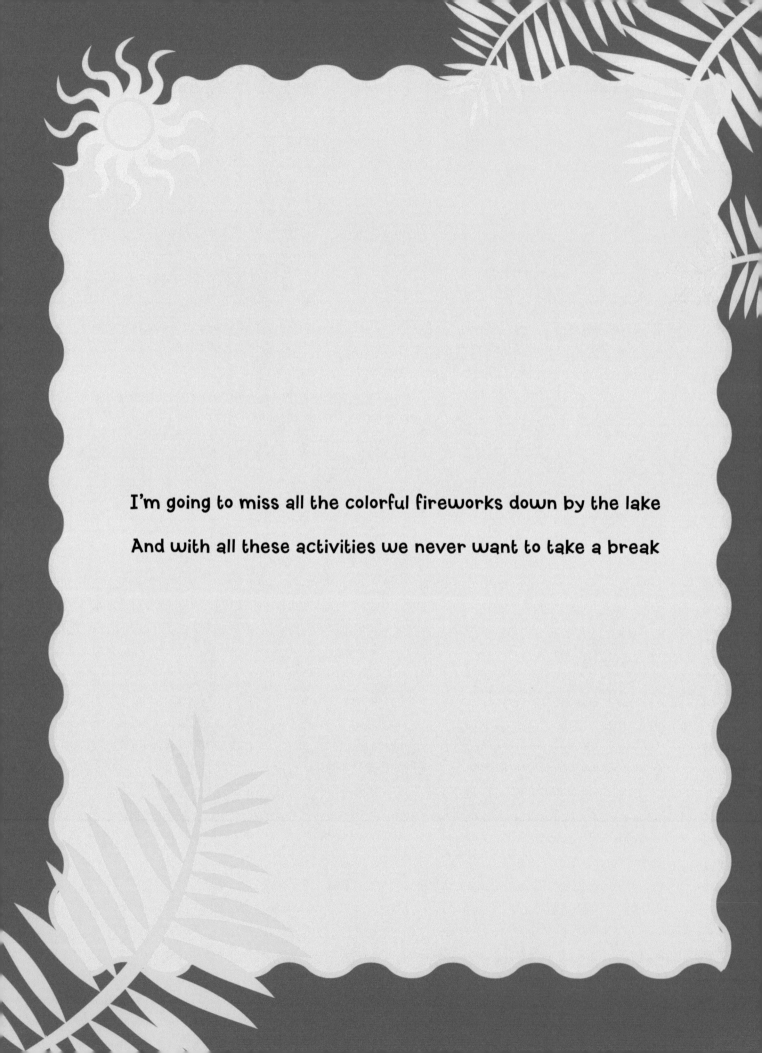

I'm going to miss all the colorful fireworks down by the lake

And with all these activities we never want to take a break

Remember the announcer yelling, "Batter up!!" at the baseball games

Calling them up one by one, name by name

Seeing all the animals at the zoo puts a smile on my face

The monkeys swinging from the trees while
watching the rabbit and turtle race

Oh how we're going to miss the summer fun

Riding rides in the sunny summer sun!

All of those delicious cakes, cookies and pies

Jumping around in the sack race and winning first prize

I'm going to miss every moment we shared together

Playing and relaxing in the warm fair weather

Mom and Dad this list can go on and on....

But tell me, what happens when the summer is gone?

My dear children can't you see,

during the summer we just let you be.

And while this season is
coming to an end

We wait with great anticipation
for the school year to begin.

ACKNOWLEDGEMENTS

We are grateful for our families and friends who traveled this journey with us. We hope this book will be something you will cherish and read to your little ones.

Printed in the United States
By Bookmasters